WORDs

Understand their power. Learn to use their strength.

HUGS

FUNNY

SWEET?

SMART

PLAYING

SMART TRYING

GIVING

Written by Linda Ragsdale   Illustrated by Imodraj

May you fill yourself with kind words and always remember to make your words count.

Designed by Flowerpot Press
in Franklin, TN.
www.FlowerpotPress.com
Designer: Stephanie Meyers
Editor: Ashley Rideout
DJS-0909-0146
ISBN: 978-1-4867-0869-7
Made in China/Fabriqué en Chine

There is nothing a Peace Dragon likes better than teaching and learning about peace.

Words are a key to peace, and we learn all about them in the pages of this book.

So come on inside...it's peaceful in here.

If an angry word heads your way, move to the side.
Mean words don't work if they miss their mark.

Call yourself SMART for stepping out of the way.

If a hateful word tries to snag your ears, close them, and hum a fun song.
Mean words don't get in if you don't pay attention.

Call yourself a CHAMPION for singing your own tune.

If a harsh word stings a friend, send a nice word their way.
A nice word can heal the hurt.

Call yourself HERO for making someone feel strong.

If a mean word should happen to sneak its way through
and become a mean spark,
boiling, and spoiling, and spewing its way out of you...

...then take your KIND words and use them to cool and calm the burn.

Call yourself HUMAN because it happens to everyone.

Fill yourself with kind words...
by the handful,
by the head-full,
by the heart-full.

Then give them away...

...in a wish, in a whisper, in a "WAHOO!"

Call yourself FRIEND, because kind words
are gifts that brighten everyone's day.

Words have a power only you can control.

They can heal or hurt, build or burn.

It's not what they say to you that matters—
it's what you say to others,
and what you say to yourself.

FUNNY

It's what you call others,
and what you call yourself.

Make your words count.

Hi! I'm Pax. I'm a Peace Dragon.

My very favorite thing in the entire world is to fly around the world and encourage people to be peacemakers, like in these books. Did you know that everyone can be a peacemaker? If you choose to see, speak, and act through a kind heart and calm thoughts, YOU are a peacemaker! Once you practice, it's easy—and pretty fun, too!

We all have times where we need help choosing peace, such as learning to work with people who are different than we are, or dealing with unkind words that come our way. By reading and thinking about ways to choose kindness or peace before a challenge comes our way, it helps us be prepared to choose peace.

By practicing awesome peaceful solutions, we become examples of love, while building a foundation of peacemaking that will last a lifetime.

HUGS,

Pax

HOW TO ENJOY THIS BOOK:

Words are powerful tools we all use every day. It's important for us to think about how our words affect those around us.

In this story, can you think of a time where words were helpful? What about hurtful? Flip back through the pictures and notice the ways words were used.

Activity time:

As a group, make a list of positive words that would be helpful to share with friends. Try to fill a board or piece of paper with beautiful words! Look back through the book to see if there are any to add.

Distribute latex-free adhesive bandages and washable ink pens to each child. Encourage children to write a favorite positive word on each bandage. Take turns sharing the kind words each person picked.

Keep the box of kind-word bandages so children can hand them out when friends might need them. When a bandage is taken out, have children to make a new one to add to the box.

Taking it further:
Challenge everyone to be on the lookout for times they could share kind words with others. If they see a friend hurt by stinging words, encourage them to extend a bandage, a kind word, or a hand to those friends. Invite parents and friends to continue the discussion of kind words when they see acts of kindness.

Learning through play:

Have each child make a paper airplane.
On the airplanes, encourage children to write kind words like those that are in the book.

Write the words "Mean Words" on a piece of paper. Place the Mean Words paper on the ground, and let the children throw their airplanes past the mean words, showing children that kind words go further than mean ones.

Talk about how when something feels frustrating, going beyond mean words by taking the time to create kind words is always the right answer.

Taking it further:
Ask each child to take their airplane home and tell their family what they learned about the importance of kind words. Encourage them to hang their airplane in their room where they can see it each day, maybe near a window or air vent where it will blow in the breeze, to remind them how far-reaching kind words can be.

HOW TO MAKE A PEACE DRAGON:

Let's draw Pax! Notice how each line on the Peace Dragon looks like a shape or letter you may already know. Each pink line is a new line you add to your drawing. See where the line starts and ends, and then draw it on your paper.

What strength would your Peace Dragon bring to the world?